THE EXTRAORDINARY FILES

Day of Judgement

Paul Blum

'The truth is inside us.
It is the only place where it can hide.'

nasen
Helping Everyone Achieve
■■■■ nasen
NASEN House, 4/5 Amber Business Village, Ar
Amington, Tamworth, Staffordshire B77 4RP

Rising Stars UK Ltd.
22 Grafton Street, London W1S 4EX
www.risingstars-uk.com

Published 2007

Cover design: Button plc
Illustrator: Aleksandar Sotiroski
Text design and typesetting: pentacor**big**
Publisher: Gill Budgell
Editor: Maoliosa Kelly
Editorial consultants: Lorraine Petersen and Cliff Moon

British Library Cataloguing in Publication Data.
A CIP record for this book is available from the British Library.

ISBN: 978-1-84680-251-5

Printed by Craft Print International Limited, Singapore

CHAPTER ONE

The oil rig was in the Arctic, 100 miles from the North Pole. The oil rig workers worked in temperatures of minus 40 degrees. There was lots of money to be made here. The oil belonged to Russia and it was the richest oil field in the world.

The oil rig workers looked up at the strange red
light in the sky. It was not beautiful, like the aurora.
The workers were frightened. They thought it was a

terrible warning that the world was about to end and that the Day of Judgement was near.

One day, as the workers looked up at the red sky they saw a terrifying sight. Four horsemen were riding above them on black horses. Behind the horsemen there was a wall of water, like a tidal wave. The wave hit the oil rig and all the workers died.

CHAPTER TWO

Robert Parker and Laura Turnbull were British Secret Service Agents who worked for MI5. Their helicopter landed in a small Russian airport in the middle of Siberia. They got out. They had lots of bags with them.

"It feels strange, working with the Russian Secret Service," said Parker. "They used to be our enemies."

"But they are our friends now," said Turnbull. "We must work together to find out what is behind these terrible tidal waves."

A man came to meet them. "My name is General Tomsky," he said. "I work for the Russian Secret Service. I am here to help you. Any information you want, I will give you."

"Great!" said Turnbull. "Sometimes the only way we can get information is to get nasty."

"I cannot believe that a woman as beautiful as you could get nasty," said General Tomsky.

Agent Turnbull went red. Then she got angry. "Listen, general," she said, "I'm not just a pretty face. I'm a professional. I'm sure a Russian Secret Service Agent like you can learn to behave like a professional, too."

They went to a small Russian hotel.

"You will have a room here," General Tomsky said. "This will be your base. Until tomorrow, Agents Turnbull and Parker."

The two agents unpacked their bags. Parker unpacked a computer and some electronic equipment. Turnbull unpacked her clothes. "We're here to look at ice and snow," said Parker. "Not to go to parties. Why do you need all those clothes?"

"Shut up, Parker. I need to look smart at all times.
Besides, I need things to cheer me up while I'm here.
It's not exactly a five-star hotel," said Turnbull.

The next day, General Tomsky took them out onto the ice cap. He showed them a map.

"All the oil rigs on this coast have been destroyed by the tidal waves," he said. "Ten thousand workers have died. My government has lost millions of pounds."

"Before the wave comes, do the workers always see four horsemen?" Parker asked.

"Yes. They believe that they're seeing the Four Horsemen of the Apocalypse," said General Tomsky, "which is a sign that the world is about to end, that the Day of Judgement is near."

"There must be another explanation for the terrible floods," said Turnbull.

"Yes. Like global warming," said Parker. "The ice caps may be melting too fast. There may be something seriously wrong with the environment here."

Parker set up a satellite probe on his computer.

"There's a space storm above Russia," he said, looking at the computer screen.

"What's a space storm?" asked Turnbull.

"A space storm is full of heat," said Parker. "The heat lights up the sky. That's why the aurora light is so strong. No wonder the sea is all shaken up."

"Is Russia in danger?" asked General Tomsky.

"Not just Russia, the whole world," Parker replied.

"We must report back to London at once," Turnbull said to Parker.

CHAPTER THREE

MI5 Headquarters, Vauxhall, London

The two agents went back to London. Their boss, Commander Watson, was very interested in their report.

"I want you to follow up every lead on this case," he told them.

As soon as they had gone, he made a phone call. "Agents Parker and Turnbull are getting too close," was all he said.

Meanwhile, Agents Parker and Turnbull went to the British Library to look up information about the Day of Judgement.

Parker was looking at a Bible when he suddenly got very excited. "The last book in the Bible is called the Book of Revelation," he said.

"It's all about the Day of Judgement."

19

"Go on," said Turnbull.

"It says that on the Day of Judgement there will be four horsemen. They will bring illness, war, starvation and death. These four things will end the world."

Turnbull scratched her head. "But do you think that the tidal waves are a sign that the world is about to end?" she asked.

"I don't know for sure," he said. "But we know that global warming is melting the ice caps. We know that sea levels are rising. Maybe we're much closer to the end of the world than we think."

"You're making me feel nervous," Turnbull replied.

"You haven't got time to feel nervous," he said. "We've got places to go, people to see. Go home and pack, Laura. We're leaving tonight."

"Oh no," she said. "Where are we going?"

"We're going to see a holy man," he said. "I'll tell you more later."

CHAPTER FOUR

The two agents went by plane to Athens in Greece.
Then they took a boat to the island of Patmos.

A taxi took them up a mountain to a very old church.

"This is the church of Saint John," Parker said. "The monks of Patmos live here. We've come to see Brother John, a famous holy man. He may be able to tell us more about the secrets of the Book of Revelation. It's said that he can see into the future."

"But why did we have to come all this way to visit him, Robert?" asked Turnbull. "Wouldn't a phone call have done?"

"The monks of Patmos have no phones. They're cut off from the outside world," said Parker.

"I hope we don't have to stay for a long time," she said, looking at the old church. "It's too quiet here for me!"

Agent Parker rang the old bell. A monk came to the door.

"We need to see Brother John," Parker said. "It's a matter of life and death."

The monk took them into a dark room,
full of candles and statues.
Brother John was lying in a bed.
He looked very old and very ill.

"Greetings, my children," he said.
"I knew you would come."

"Brother John, we need your help.
Can you look into the future and tell us
if the world is in danger?" Parker said.
"Some people say they have seen the
Four Horsemen of the Apocalypse."

"Then it is true," said Brother John, with
a sigh. "The Day of Judgement is near,"
said Brother John. "Now I can believe
the dream that I have had for the last
three nights."

"Tell us your dream," said Agent Turnbull.

"In my dream I see boats and boxes," the old man said. "The boxes are in the shape of stars. I see ice. I see the Sun. I see a big lake. I see the sunlight shining into the lake. The water is on fire. It turns red – so red. Then the ice melts into water. The water is fast and strong. Great waves hit the land. The whole of the earth is drowned. The four horsemen come to take the living and the dead."

Both agents felt a shiver go down their spines.

"Thank you, Brother John," said Agent Parker. He could see that the old man was very tired after telling his story.

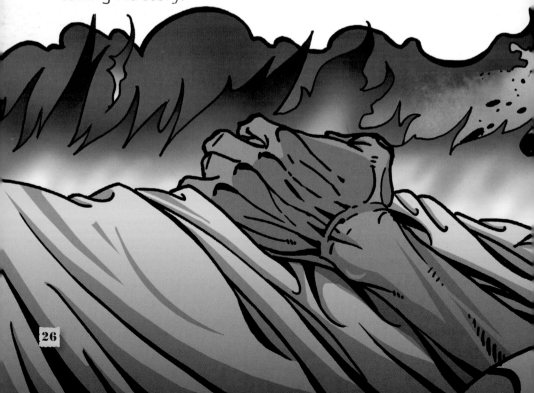

CHAPTER FIVE

MI5 Headquarters, Vauxhall, London

The two agents went back to London. They worked all night looking for clues that might explain Brother John's dream.

"In Brother John's dream there were boats and boxes shaped like stars," said Turnbull. "What could that mean?"

"I think I've got it!" said Parker suddenly. "Do you remember Operation Mirrors?"

"The American project that was dropped? As far as I remember, they planned to put mirrors into outer space. The mirrors were supposed to reflect the Sun's rays back on itself. It was a brilliant plan to stop global warming," said Turnbull.

"But don't you remember, Laura? The mirrors were shaped like stars!" said Parker.

Suddenly, Parker jumped up with excitement.

"That's it!" he shouted. "Operation Mirrors wasn't dropped. It's still on the go. They're packing those mirrors into boxes and putting them into big boats. That's what Brother John's dream was about."

"Where could they be doing this?" asked Turnbull.

"Southampton docks is the only place big enough to do that," said Parker.

"Let's go!" said Turnbull.

The two agents drove to Southampton.

The docks were very spooky at night. They drove around for a while then Agent Turnbull saw something incredible.

"Wow, Parker, look at that!" she said.

They saw a massive star-shaped box. It was as big as a football pitch.

"We need to find out where that's going," said Parker.

Before the two agents could do anything, they were
surrounded by soldiers.

They were taken to a dark office. In a chair, sat a man wearing glasses. They couldn't see his face, but Parker and Turnbull knew that they had seen this man before.

"Congratulations, Agents Parker and Turnbull," he said. "You are about to be rewarded for your brilliant detective work. You found out about Operation Mirrors and now you will become a part of it."

"What is Operation Mirrors, Agent X?" asked Turnbull.

"I see you remember my name," he said. "Operation Mirrors is a plan to stop the warming of the planet. It will use mirrors to reflect the light back onto the Sun."

"You two agents are going into space to see if the project is working."

"But how will we get back to Earth?" asked Parker.

X just laughed. "Agents Parker and Turnbull, I will leave that for you to work out."

They put Parker and Turnbull into a rocket. Then they fired them into space.

"OK, I'm really scared but this is fantastic!" said Turnbull.

"Look at those giant star-shaped mirrors," said Parker. "They're catching the sunlight. The sky looks just like Brother John described."

Then Parker's face froze with horror.

"What's wrong, Robert?" asked Turnbull.

"Look carefully, Laura," he said. "The mirrors aren't sending the sunlight back to the Sun. They're sending it down onto the Earth."

"You're right, Parker," she said. "What is going on?"

"The Americans are sending down the sunlight onto Northern Russia. They're trying to melt the ice!" Parker shouted.

"But why would they do that?" Turnbull said.

"They want to flood the Russian oil fields. They want to stop Russia becoming richer than America," Parker replied. "Now we know what Operation Mirrors is really about."

"We'll never be able to tell anyone what we know!" cried Turnbull. "We're in a rocket going to outer space."

"Maybe I can do something about that," said Parker. "Put on your parachute and hold on to your seat, Agent Turnbull. This might wreck your hairdo."

He pressed some buttons and the rocket began to dive back towards the Earth. The blood rushed to their heads. Agents Parker and Turnbull passed out.

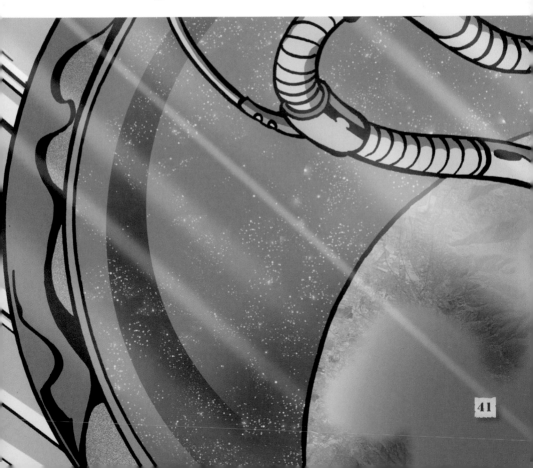

When they came to, they were floating in the air on parachutes. They landed safely in a field.

"How did we live through that?" gasped Turnbull.

"I don't know," Parker said. "Maybe the Secret Service wants us to live for some reason. I can't think why."

"We need to go and see Commander Watson once we've worked out where we are," said Turnbull.

"I think the time for going to see Commander Watson is long past," Parker said. "When we get back home, I'm going to put on my best suit."

"Parker, are you mad? You never wear a suit," Turnbull said. "You're always the scruffy one, remember?"

43

"I need to wear a suit. I'm going to the newspapers and the television studios to do an interview," said Parker. "Are you coming with me?"

She was silent. She was thinking. Then she took hold of his hand. "Robert, you're right. It's time for the ordinary people to find out about the Extraordinary Files. The truth has been silent for long enough!"

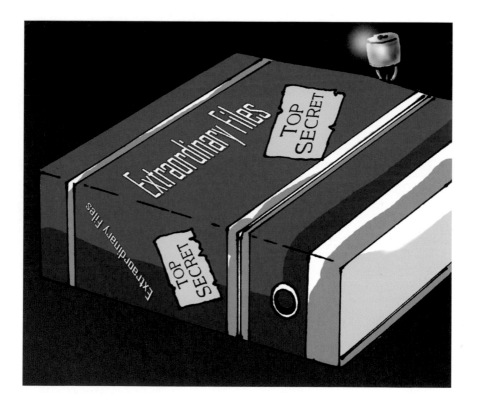

GLOSSARY OF TERMS

apocalypse an event involving great destruction and ending the world

Arctic the region around the North Pole

aurora moving, coloured lights in the sky above the North Pole

Day of Judgement the last day of the world when God will judge everyone

docks enclosed area of water where boats can be loaded and unloaded

dropped stopped

five-star hotel luxury hotel

global warming the warming up of the planet

matter of life and death something of grave importance

MI5 government department responsible for national security

on the go up and running, operational

Secret Service government department responsible for national security

tidal wave a huge wave

QUIZ

1   Where was the oil rig?

2   What did the oil rig workers see in the sky?

3   What was the name of the Russian general?

4   What are the messages of the Four Horsemen of the Apocalypse?

5   Who did the agents go to see in Greece?

6   What was the name of the American plan to stop global warming?

7   Who did the agents meet in Southampton?

8   Where did X send the agents?

9   What was the real use of Operation Mirrors?

10   Why did Parker need a suit?

ABOUT THE AUTHOR

Paul Blum has taught for over 20 years in London inner-city schools.

I wrote The Extraordinary Files for my pupils so they've been tested by some fierce critics (you!). That's why I know you'll enjoy reading them.

I've made the stories edgy in terms of character and content and I've written them using the kind of fast-paced dialogue you'll recognise from television soaps. I hope you find The Extraordinary Files an interesting and easy-to-read collection of stories.

ANSWERS TO QUIZ

1 In the Arctic

2 The Four Horsemen of the Apocalypse

3 General Tomsky

4 Illness, war, starvation, death

5 Brother John

6 Operation Mirrors

7 X

8 Into outer space in a rocket

9 To flood the Russian oil fields

10 To go to the newspapers and television studios to do an interview